W9-CIN-548

Yussel's Prayer

A YOM KIPPUR STORY

Retold by Barbara Cohen
Illustrated by Michael J. Deraney

Lothrop, Lee & Shepard Books / New York

 Inquiries should be addressed to Lothrop, Lee & Shepard Books, a division of William Morrow & Company, Inc., 105 Madison Avenue, New York, New York 10016. Printed in the United States of America. First Edition. 2 3 4 5 6 7 8 9 10

Library of Congress Cataloging in Publication Data
Cohen, Barbara./Yussel's prayer./Summary: A cowherd's simple but sincere Yom Kippur prayer is instrumental in ending the day's fast./[1. Prayers–Fiction. 2. Yom Kippur–Fiction. 3. Fasts and feasts–Judaism–Fiction] I. Deraney, Michael J. II. Title. PZ7.C6595Yu [Fic] 80-25377 ISBN 0-688-00460-1
ISBN 0-688-00461-X (lib. bdg.)

For Rabbi Ronald Isaacs,
with affection and gratitude
B.C.

To my mother and father,
with love
M.J.D.

It was Yom Kippur, the Day of Atonement. All the people who lived in the village were on their way to the shul to pray. There they would remain for the entire day, fasting, beating their breasts, and asking God to forgive all their sins.

All the people, that is, except one. Yussel, the orphan boy who slept in Reb Meir's dairy barn, rose at dawn as usual. He didn't know much, for no one had ever taught him anything, but he knew that this was a special day.

He stood in the courtyard and waited for Reb Meir to come out of his great house. He didn't have to wait long. Reb Meir and his sons always left early for shul. They wore long black coats, lined with fur, and big fur hats.

Yussel tugged at Reb Meir's wide sleeve. "Excuse me, Reb Meir," he whispered.

From his great height, Reb Meir looked down at Yussel. "Yes?" he asked.

"Please, Reb Meir, may I go to shul today? May I go and pray like everyone else?"

"No," Reb Meir replied. His voice was not unkind, but it was very firm. "The cows must be taken to pasture today. The cows don't know it's Yom Kippur. You must do your job, as you do any other time."

"Besides," scoffed Reb Meir's eldest son, "what good would it do you to go to shul? You can't read. So how can you understand the prayer book? How can you pray?"

Reb Meir and his sons walked out through their wide gate. Yussel watched as they made their way down the street toward the shul. He watched until he could no longer see even a dot of black in the distance.

Then he returned to the barn. He called softly to the cows. They came when he called them, as they always did.

He picked up the little pipe he had made from a reed he had found growing by the river. Holding the pipe in his hand, he led the cows out to pasture. He didn't stop first at Reb Meir's kitchen to beg a piece of black bread from the cook, as he usually did. It was Yom Kippur, and if he couldn't pray, at least he could fast.

Reb Meir and his sons sat in the seats of honor, the seats by the eastern wall of the synagogue. Of all the people in the congregation, they were seated nearest their holy rabbi, who was known far and wide for his loving kindness and his deeds of charity. Some of the rabbi's followers even believed that he spoke directly to God, as had Abraham and Moses long ago.

Reb Meir's lips formed the words of the prayers. According to tradition, he beat his breast with his fist when he and everyone else in the room together confessed their sins. But his mind wasn't on the words he was saying, or the gestures he was making.

"If I can buy a thousand bushels of grain in Lublin next week," he was thinking as he said the prayers, "I can store it in my barns until deep winter sets in, and sell it then at a great profit. I wonder," his mind said as his fist struck his chest, "I wonder how much the farmers at the Lublin market will ask for their grain this year, and I wonder how much less I can give them than they ask."

Reb Meir's eldest son formed the words of the prayers too. He also beat his breast with his fist. But he wasn't thinking about the words of the Yom Kippur service either. He was thinking instead about asking his father to let him make a trip to Warsaw.

"It's so dull in this little town," he thought to himself. "In Warsaw there are fine shops and theaters and restaurants, and beautiful women everywhere. I think," his mind said as his fist struck his chest, "I think I'll go to Warsaw whether my father likes it or not!"

All day Reb Meir and his sons fasted and prayed. All day they prayed and fasted. The day seemed endless. There were many moments when instead of praying to God to forgive their sins they prayed for darkness to come.

At long last, through the window, they saw the sun sinking low in

the west. Yom Kippur was almost over. Soon their holy rabbi would begin the final prayers. Then they could go home and break their day-long fast with herring and boiled potatoes. Their mouths watered. Already they could taste the black bread spread with yellow butter.

But, though the shadows deepened, though darkness drew nearer and nearer, the rabbi didn't begin the final prayers. He didn't begin the closing service. He didn't ask God to shut the gates of heaven and seal the congregation in the Book of Life.

Instead he chanted hymn after hymn and recited prayer after prayer, still begging God to listen to the words of those gathered in the shul, to listen to the words of all those celebrating Yom Kippur everywhere.

Reb Meir began to get angry. What was the matter with the rabbi? Why didn't he end the service? It had gone on long enough. It was dark out. The sun had long since sunk below the horizon. There were three stars in the sky. It was time to be done with Yom Kippur.

If the Rabbi didn't begin Ne'lah, the closing service, in two minutes, Reb Meir decided he and his sons were going to walk out of the shul anyway!

In the pasture, the day had been a long one too. The cows had grazed as usual, but Yussel had eaten nothing. He hadn't even gone down to the river to get a drink of water. He had sat in the sunshine, thinking. The evening drew near, and the shadows lengthened.

As the sun sank in the west, he picked up his reed pipe.

"O God," he cried, "I don't know any prayers. But I do know how to play the pipe. Since I can't give you any words, I give you this tune instead."

On his pipe, Yussel began playing a melody that he had made up himself.

While he played it, he gazed at the thick grass growing all around him, at the great sky above him, at the cows grazing peacefully before him, and he thought about the goodness of God.

His mind, his soul, his heart were all in the music he played for God as the sun set below the horizon and three stars appeared in the sky.

And at that moment, at that very moment, in the shul, the rabbi began to chant the Ne'lah prayers.

"Our Father, our King," he cried, his voice full of joy, "seal us in the Book of Life. Seal us there for a year of health and prosperity."

And then he picked up the shofar, the ram's horn, and blew a loud, clear blast that echoed in every corner of the room. Yom Kippur was over.

"Thank goodness," thought Reb Meir. "About time," thought his sons. But to each other, and to all the other members of the congregation, they murmured, "L'shana tova–a good year."

Reb Meir went forward to greet the rabbi. A crowd pressed around him, but they separated to make way for Reb Meir.

"L'shana tova, Rabbi," said Reb Meir.

"L'shana tova, Reb Meir," said the rabbi.

"I have a question," Reb Meir said. He was the only one who dared to ask it, although the very same question was in the mind of every person in the shul.

"Why did you wait so long to begin Ne'lah? Why did you wait so long to bring Yom Kippur to an end?"

The rabbi looked straight into Reb Meir's eyes. "I had a vision," he said. "In my vision I saw that the gates of heaven were closed. Our prayers weren't reaching God. Our prayers weren't acceptable to Him."

"Why?" asked Reb Meir.

The rabbi shrugged. "I'm not sure," he said. "I think because they didn't come from the heart. And how could I end Yom Kippur when I felt that God wouldn't grant us forgiveness or mercy because He hadn't heard us ask for it?"

"But then you did," Reb Meir said. "Then you did end Yom Kippur."

The rabbi nodded. "I had another vision," he said. "I heard a melody, a simple melody played on a reed pipe. I saw the gates of heaven open up. All our prayers went in to God, because He had opened the gates to admit that melody."

"But why?" asked Reb Meir again. "Why just a tune on a reed pipe and not all the holy words we were saying?"

"Because," said the rabbi, "whoever sent that melody to God sent it with his whole heart. It was a true prayer."

Head down, eyes thoughtful, Reb Meir left the shul, all his sons around him. On his way home, he met Yussel, coming back from the pasture with the cows. By the light of the moon that shone above them, Reb Meir saw the little reed pipe in Yussel's hand.

"L'shana tova, Yussel," said Reb Meir.

"L'shana tova, Reb Meir," Yussel replied. He could hardly believe that the great Reb Meir was wishing him a good year.

"Will you come into my house, Yussel?" Reb Meir asked. "Will you break the fast with me and my family?"

"Father!" exclaimed Reb Meir's eldest son. "He's so dirty and so ragged. How can you let him in the house?"

"Very easily," said Reb Meir. "Through the front door." He put his arm around Yussel's shoulders. Together they walked up the moonlit street, all of Reb Meir's sons and all of Yussel's cows trailing behind.

IN HONOR OF THE BAT MITZVAH OF
OUR DAUGHTER
LYNNE RUTH TAPPER
BY
BETSY & MAYER TAPPER
NOVEMBER 24, 1984